MOONDAY

O N D A Y

Adam Rex

Disney • HYPERION BOOKS

NEW YORK

for Little Nemo

The moon hung full and low
and touched the tips of trees.

We whispered words like *big*
and *beautiful*.

Through the backseat window
I followed its flight,

past the dark, sleeping park and
the bright empty streets.

Then I drifted to sleep and was
lifted to bed.

The next morning, the moon was lower and larger.

And very nearly on the ground.

It was in our backyard.

I asked, "Why is it so large and low?
Why is it in our backyard?"
"Huh," Dad said, and rubbed his chin.

"Pick me up."

From Dad's shoulders,
I brushed the moon with
my fingertips.

It was chalky and cold.

I climbed into a crater.

"I'm going to have a look around."

Mom said, "Okay. Zip up your coat."

I walked over
and under
and around
to where Mom and Dad waited.

Morning had missed us.
In darkness, the town
awoke and went to work.

At school we slumped in desks
and slept through lunch.
I looked through my heavy lashes,
through the window, through lean trees
to see my blue moon staring back at me.

In science, Ms. Ellen wrote,

> *The moon has gravity that makes the tides turn.*

In English, she wrote,

> *Moon is a noun. And sometimes a verb.*

In math, she wrote,

> *1 + 1 = moon,*

and then she blinked and stepped back from the board.

"That's not right," she said. "I'm sleepy. Class dismissed."

As I walked, I watched the weary townfolk.

Hushed, they shuffled through slush and dozed off at stoplights.

The band on Bleecker Street could only sigh into the microphone,

Lullaboo,
I love you,
Shush-a-loo-la,
Lullaboo.

In my backyard,
Mom and Dad tried to hide the moon under blankets and tablecloths.

"Hot air balloon?"
yawned our neighbor
as he leaned over
the fence.

"Yes . . . I guess,"
my mom said.

"It's the latest fad,"
said Dad.

That was when the tide came in.
It trickled into our backyard.
The tide came in, smooth and thin,
and settled underneath our moon.

"Big," I said. "And beautiful."

"Wet," said Dad.

"It doesn't belong in our backyard," said Mom. "And I could do without the dogs."

I said,

"Maybe we should take it for a drive."

So we drove with the moon in our window that night,
through the bright empty streets, past the dark sleeping park.
It followed our flight to the top of the hill, where it lit on the tips of the trees.

I told the moon, "Stay,"
as we rumbled away.

And it stayed in the sky
at the top of the hill,
and looked smaller and
higher the lower we drove.

"There it goes," I said.

"There goes the moon," said Dad.

"There goes our good tablecloth,"
said Mom.

In the purring car, I fell asleep.

Dad carried me to bed and said goodnight.

In other towns and neighbors' beds they said goodnight,

turned off the light,

and it was a good night everywhere.

Copyright © 2013
by Adam Rex | All rights reserved.
Published by Disney • Hyperion Books, an imprint
of Disney Book Group. No part of this book may be
reproduced or transmitted in any form or by any means,
electronic or mechanical, including photocopying, recording,
or by any information storage and retrieval system, without
written permission from the publisher. For information address
Disney • Hyperion Books, 125 West End Avenue, New York, New York
10023. | First Edition | 10 9 8 7 6 5 4 3 2 1 | H106-9333-5-13135 | Printed
in Malaysia | Library of Congress Cataloging-in-Publication Data: Rex,
Adam. Moonday / Adam Rex.—1st ed. | p. cm. | Summary: When the
Moon disrupts a town by lowering itself into a family's backyard, a
child finds a way to return the Moon to its proper place in the sky.
| ISBN 978-1-4231-1920-3 | [1. Moon—Fiction.] I. Title. II.
Title: Moon day. | PZ7.R32865Mo 2013 | [E]—dc23
2012020301 | Reinforced binding | Visit
www.disneyhyperionbooks.com